The Lost Child

A *Folktale*

by

J. Janda

Illustrated by

Christopher Fay

For the Carmelite Community

J. Janda

Paulist Press

New York/Mahwah, N.J.

Dedication

For Sister Barbara Janda

Illustrations and cover design: Christopher Fay

Book design: Saija Autrand/Faces Type & Design

Library of Congress Cataloging-in-Publication Data

Janda, J.
    The lost child / by J. Janda ; illustrated by Christopher Fay.
      p. cm.
    Summary: On a visit to Jerusalem, four-year-old Jesus gets lost, but instead of being afraid, he trusts enough in God's care to fall asleep.
    ISBN 0-8091-6646-1 (alk. paper)
    1. Jesus Christ—Juvenile fiction. [1. Jesus Christ—Fiction. 2. Lost children—Fiction.] I. Fay, Christopher L., ill. II. Title.
PZ7.J18Lo 1999
[E]—dc21
                                                   97-26240
                                                         CIP
                                                         AC

Published by Paulist Press
997 Macarthur Boulevard
Mahwah, New Jersey 07430

www.paulistpress.com

Printed and bound in Hong Kong

In Chimayo, New Mexico,
there is a statue
of the Christ Child
sitting in a chair
fast asleep.

His head is leaning
on his left hand.
His left elbow is
on the arm
of the chair.
His legs are stretched out
and crossed.
He is sound asleep.

The people of Chimayo
call this statue of Jesus
El Niño Perdido,
the Lost Child.

They have a story
that goes with it.

It is a story about Jesus
when he was
only four years old.

Jerusalem

Every year, after Jesus was born, Mary and Joseph would take him to the Temple in Jerusalem for the big feast of the Passover. The journey took about two days. Now that Jesus was four years old, he could walk by himself. When he got tired, Joseph would let him ride on the back of the donkey.

And when they got to Jerusalem, there was so much to see. There was so much to eat. There was so much to do.

Jesus always got something new when he was in Jerusalem. That year, he got a new pair of sandals, and a big hat with a bright circle in the center.

Later, Joseph surprised him and his mother with a sack of cookies made out of honey and almonds. They were Jesus' favorite cookies.

But what Jesus liked best was in the Temple yards. Animals. He spent most of his time there.

There were cages of doves that were white as snow. They looked so shy and gentle. Jesus started to talk to them.

"Are you hungry?" he asked.

Then he dropped some cookie crumbs into their cages and watched the doves peck them up.

There were baby lambs, too. Their wool felt very soft and thick.

"Can I hold this one?" Jesus asked the merchant who was selling them.

"Sure," said the merchant, "but if someone wants to buy him, you must hand him over."

So Jesus sat down in the straw and let the little lamb curl up in his lap.

A little later, he walked over to see the goats.
They were noisy.

He saw a man milking a goat. He was telling a
customer, "She is not for sale. We need the milk for
our children."

Then he saw another man pay for a goat, put a rope around its neck, and try to lead it away. He pulled and pulled, but the goat did not want to go with him.

"Are you going to take that goat back home?" asked Jesus.

"No," said the man. "I'm going to have it sacrificed."

"What does sacrifice mean?" asked Jesus, but the man did not answer him. He just kept dragging the goat away with the rope.

Then Jesus turned around to ask his parents
what the word "sacrifice" means, but they were not
there. He thought they had been looking at the
animals, too.

"I'd better look for them," he said to himself,
and walked over to the Women's Court. They were
not there.

Then he hurried over to the Men's Court, but they
were not there.

Then he ran back to where the doves and lambs
and goats were, but they were not there.

He began to worry, but then he remembered what Joseph, his father, had told him one night while they were sitting outside watching the stars. "Son, look at all those stars," he had said. "God made each one, and the moon, too. Now if God can do that, he can take care of you. That is why you must never worry or be afraid. If you do, just look up at the sky and tell yourself, 'If God can make all those stars, and take such good care of them, then God can take care of me.'"

Jesus was feeling very tired. His feet were sore, and he was hungry. Then he said to himself, "If God can make all the stars, and take such good care of them, then God can take care of me. I'm too tired to keep running around and looking for my parents. This is enough. God will find them for me."

Then Jesus saw an open door.
When he walked over and
looked inside, he saw an
empty room with
empty chairs.
He went inside,
sat down on
one of the
chairs, and
soon fell
fast asleep.

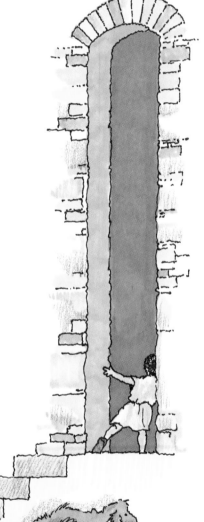

Mary and Joseph

Are you wondering where Mary and Joseph were, and what they were thinking? Well, Mary thought Jesus was with Joseph, and Joseph thought Jesus was with Mary. When they met, Joseph said to Mary, "Where is Jesus? I thought he was with you."

But Mary said, "I thought he was with you."

Then they both said, "But he is not!" Then they ran all over looking for Jesus.

They looked in
the Women's Court,
but he was not there.
They looked in the
Men's Court, but he
was not there. They
looked around the
place where the
animals were being
sold, but he was
not there.

Mary started to cry.

Just then, that man who let Jesus hold the lamb saw Mary crying.

"Are you looking for a little boy?" he asked.

"Yes," said Mary.

"Is he about this tall?" asked the man.

"Yes," they said.

"Does he like animals?" asked the man.

"Yes," said Mary. "Where is he? I'm his mother. Please, tell me where he is."

"Well," said the man, "I saw him wandering over there, near that open door. I think he went inside."

"Where?" asked Joseph. "Near what open door?"

Then the man pointed to the door he saw Jesus enter, and he said, "There."

Well, before the man could turn his head, Mary and Joseph were halfway there.

Jesus Is Found

They were out of breath as they ran through the door and into the room. Suddenly, they stopped. They saw a circle of old priests. There, in the middle of them, was Jesus—sound asleep in a chair. His head was resting on his left hand. His left elbow was on the arm of the chair. His legs were stretched out and crossed. He looked very happy and peaceful.

Don't Wake Him Just Yet

"May I help you?" asked one of the old priests.

"That is our son," said Mary. "We have been looking all over for him."

Then as Mary rushed over to Jesus, the same priest touched her arm and said, "Don't wake him just yet."

"But why?" asked Mary.

"Because," said the priest, "he is the wisest person we have ever seen."

"And why do you say that?" asked his mother.

"Because when he is tired, he sleeps. Nowadays, all people do is run around. All people do is worry. What for? God is in charge. Look at you—you are all nervous and upset. Why?"

Well, of course Mary knew that the priest was right. At first she was embarrassed, but then she started to laugh. Then Joseph laughed, and soon everybody in the room was laughing.

Just then, Jesus woke up to find everybody laughing. And Jesus started to laugh, too.

When Mary saw Jesus laughing, she asked him, "What's so funny?"

"Oh, I don't know," answered Jesus. "But everybody else is laughing, so I thought I'd laugh too."

Then all those in the room started laughing again, and they couldn't stop till their sides ached.

After some time, Jesus said, "I'm hungry. Let's eat." So Mary and Joseph each took one of his hands and walked back to the caravan. They had a good supper.

Then they all went into their tent, lay down, and fell fast asleep.

And that is the story
of the Lost Child.